Bye, Bye, Butterfree

By Diane Muldrow

Illustrated by DRI Artworks

A GOLDEN BOOK®
Golden Books Publishing Company, Inc.
New York, NY 10106

One sunny day, as Ash, Pikachu, Misty, and Brock made their way to a new city and a new gym, they paused at a cliff ledge to look out at the sea.

"Hey, what are those?" asked Ash, pointing up at the sky.

"They look like Butterfree!" said Misty.

"This is the season when Butterfree find mates," said Brock. "Then they fly across the sea to lay their eggs."

Ash gulped, and said, "You mean my Butterfree would go, too?"

"If you don't let it cross the sea, it will never have babies," Brock replied.

Ash and his friends decided to rent a hot air balloon to get close to the Butterfree, as many other Butterfree trainers were doing. Soon the friends were quickly floating in the air, going higher and higher!

"Hold on, guys!" said Brock.

"Wow!" said Ash. "What a view!"

"Look!" said Misty. "All the Butterfree are pairing off!"

"Any time now, Ash," hinted Brock.

"Right!" said Ash, as he threw the Poké ball.
"Butterfree, Go!"
   Butterfree emerged from the ball, and looked at
Ash curiously.
   "Go out there and find your mate!" coaxed Ash.
   "Good luck, Butterfree!" called Misty.

As Ash and his friends held their breath,
Butterfree looked around at all the other
Butterfree. Then it finally flew over to one that was
still by itself.

"Butterfree found someone it likes!" said Ash happily. "Yeah, it's love at first sight with that pink one," said Brock. Butterfree fluttered and danced around the pink Butterfree. But the pink Butterfree wanted nothing to do with poor Butterfree.

"Butterfree!" called Ash. "Have confidence in yourself! Show it your whirlwind attack!"

Butterfree showed off its strength, but the pink Butterfree was still not impressed.

"Pika, pika," said Pikachu sadly.

As they all wondered how to help Butterfree, they noticed a helicopter speeding toward the Butterfree swarm.

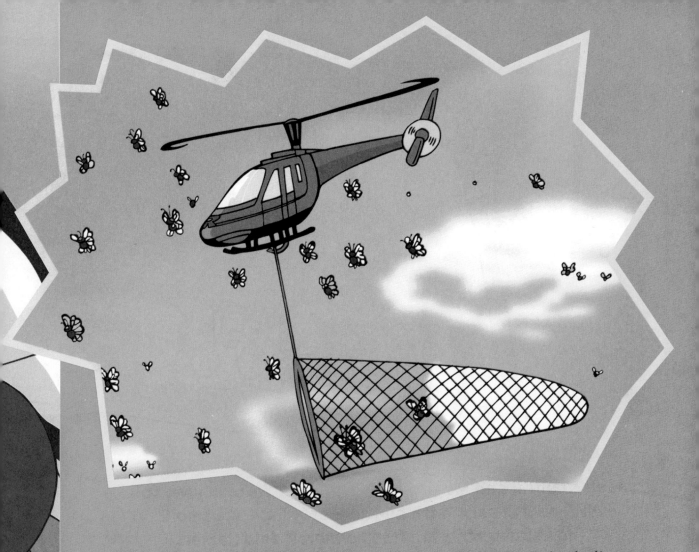

It had a big red R on the door. Ash realized that the helicopter belonged to . . . Team Rocket!

Out from the bottom of the helicopter came a giant net. It began to scoop up hundreds of Butterfree!

"Stop!" cried Brock over the noise of the helicopter propellers. "You're going to disrupt their whole egg-laying season!"

"Can't you see these Butterfree are in love?" shouted Misty.

Jessie, James, and Meowth only laughed. "We're in love, too, little girl," said Jessie, "with all the pretty little Pokémon!"

"Those Butterfree are free no more!" said James.

Butterfree flew quickly over to the net. The pink Butterfree had been caught! It looked at Butterfree sadly through net.

Butterfree did a brave tackle attack on the Team Rocket chopper.

"That pathetic little insect thinks it can stop us," said Jessie.

"Butterfree, stun spore now!" called Ash.

Butterfree flew above the helicopter and tried to shower down its stun spore — but the revolving blades just blew it away from the chopper.

Team Rocket turned and headed in another direction. They were getting away!

Butterfree followed the chopper as fast as it could.

Eventually Ash and his friends found Butterfree waiting for them. Butterfree led them down to a deep canyon where, in a warehouse, Team Rocket had hidden their stolen Butterfree.

"What a great catch!" said James as he looked at the net stuffed with Butterfree.

Just then, Team Rocket heard some glass breaking.

"Hey — somebody's bustin' in!" cried Meowth.

"Who is it? Who's there?" cried Jessie.

Ash and his friends broke through the window!
"Prepare for trouble!" announced Ash.
"And you can make that triple!" added Misty.
"We're defending the beauty of truth and love!"
"Butterfree, go!" cried Ash, hurling the Poké ball.

"Starmie, tackle attack!" ordered Misty.
And the battle for the Butterfree began.

As the pink Butterfree watched hopefully, Butterfree attacked the net again and again. But it wasn't able to tear it.

Finally, summoning all its strength, Butterfree hit it one more time — and tore a big hole through the net!

The Butterfree were free at last!

"Take this!" cried Jessie, swinging at Starmie. She managed to stun Starmie.

But Misty easily revived Starmie with water, and soon Starmie was ready to battle.

Meanwhile, Brock opened the door of the warehouse.

"Hurry up! Fly away!" he cried, as the Butterfree quickly escaped.

Team Rocket was determined to get back the Butterfree. They managed to get back into their helicopter — and it didn't take them long to catch up to the Butterfree swarm.

Ash, Pikachu, Misty and Brock rushed back to their hot air balloon and took off in the air after Team Rocket.

Now it was Pikachu's turn to help the Butterfree. Pikachu hopped on Butterfree's back, and together they flew over to the Team Rocket helicopter.

Brave little Pikachu jumped off Butterfree's back, and landed on the chopper.

Team Rocket gasped in fear.

"It's going to shock us! It's going to shock us!" they cried.

With Pikachu's powerful Thundershock attack, Team Rocket was soon blasting off again!

Now the pink Butterfree was dancing for Butterfree!
"All right!" said Ash. "Good for you, Butterfree!"
But inside, Ash felt sad. He knew that it was now time
for Butterfree to leave him, and fly across the ocean with
the pink Butterfree.

Ash knelt down to talk to Butterfree, who was also feeling sad. "Don't worry, Butterfree," said Ash softly. "I'll just tell all the other Pokémon that you're on a trip — and that you'll come back someday. Good-bye, Butterfree."

As the two Butterfree took off together into the sky, Ash thought about all the wonderful times he'd had with Butterfree, as they'd traveled from town to town.

"Good-bye, Butterfree! I'll always remember you — thank you for everything!"called Ash, as the Butterfree disappeared into the sunset.

Brock put his hand on Ash's shoulder. "Ash, you raised Butterfree to have a lot of courage, " he said. "And I think you just proved that you have lots of courage, too."

Good friendships last forever, even though friends don't always stay together. Helping Butterfree to grow, Ash just may have also grown himself!